Matthew,

I hope your
Dreams
Send you Soaring.

Jacqueline
Leigh

To my lovely Grandma Shirley, whose encouraging, kind, and loving support throughout my life and especially now has made grand feats possible. The greatest accomplishment of all may be witnessing you, Gigi, share the story of Ford & Red with your many great-grandchildren.

www.mascotbooks.com

Time For Bed with Ford & Red

For more information, please contact:
Mascot Books
560 Herndon Parkway #120
Herndon, VA 20170
info@mascotbooks.com

Library of Congress Control Number: 2017902785

CPSIA Code: PRT0417B
ISBN-13: 978-1-63177-985-5

Printed in the United States

TIME FOR BED
WITH FORD & RED

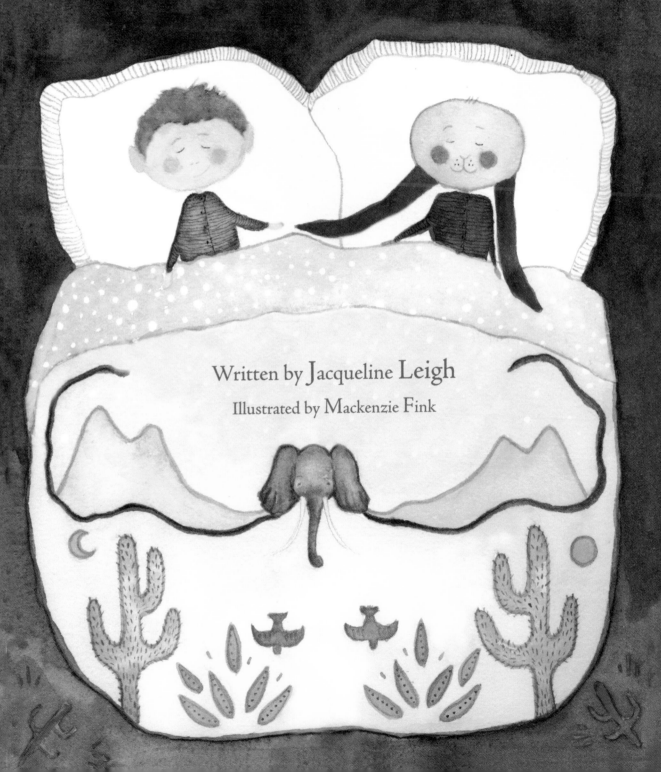

Written by Jacqueline Leigh

Illustrated by Mackenzie Fink

Mom tucks me in and turns out the light.
My bunny Red and I snuggle together all night.
We're deep in hushed slumber as our dreams begin.
Red and I hold tight for a hoot-howlin' spin.

We gallop with cowboys across the land.
"I'm Ford!" I shout, as I hold Red's hand.

Red tips his hat and yells
out a "Howdy!"
Then saddles his horse and
rides loud and rowdy.

The bucks are set loose, running wild in the mud.
They knock Red off his horse, and he lands with a thud!
I rope 'em, and tie 'em, and ride 'em in stride,
I'm rip-roarin' Ford, the giddyup guide.

Uh-oh Red, we need to sweep.
Our bed is dusty from that rough-ridin' sleep!
What happens next in the world we dream?
Just close your eyes, I bet it's extreme.

We dive with dolphins in the salty sea.
They swim and splash between Red and me.

We catch their fins and
hitch us a ride,
Exploring the ocean with
our friendly guides.

A fishing net drops from a ship overhead,
Tangling a baby whale in each tricky thread.
Red tugs at the net with all of his might,
So the baby and his mama can reunite.

My sheets are soaked from that soggy dream.
That's it, Red! No more oceans or streams.
What happens next in the world we dream?
Just close your eyes, I bet it's extreme.

Red and I whip through the bright sky,
Our mighty blue capes are flying high.
We spot a rainbow surrounded by clouds,
And settle on top of it, standing proud.

A gust of wind
spins us around.
We tumble and fall and
zoom toward the ground.

But an eagle swoops in
to save the day.
He guides us home,
then soars away.

Snug in my bed with my cape tied tight,
I'm snoozing and snoring, dreaming of flight.
What happens next in the world we dream?
Just close your eyes, I bet it's extreme.

We go on safari in prickly heat.
A watering hole will cool off our feet.
We're rolling in mud and stomping in muck.
I'm covered in filth and feeling like yuck!

Red climbs up on an elephant's tusk,
And they search for food from dawn until dusk.
Juicy green pears will taste just right.
The elephant gives Red a yummy bite.

Look at that elephant, all happy and fed.
He's tucked in tight, cuddling Red.

Morning comes, and I'm well rested.
I stayed in my bed just like mom requested.
"Red," I hum, "morning is here."
He and the elephant rise with cheer.

We plop at the table for morning treats.
A tasty meal that even the elephant eats!
Dust falls from Red's ear, sprinkling his tea.
He whispers, "Yee-haw," and winks at me.

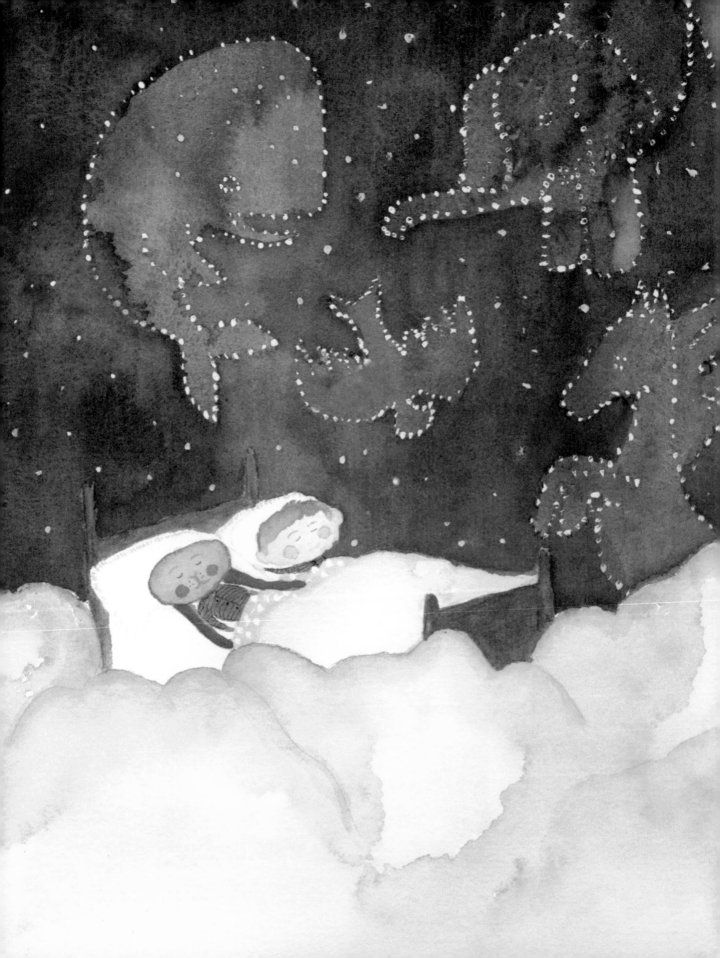

So you see, lots can happen when daytime ends,
As we doze and dream with our favorite friends.

Meet the Author

Jacqueline Leigh holds a BA in Journalism from Valdosta State University. She's successfully published articles in multiple magazines and online publications. She's perfected her craft by blending her affection for writing with the thrill of entertaining our youth. Jacqueline makes her home among the dogwood trees with her husband and two spirited children.

About the Illustrator

Mackenzie Fink is a freelance illustrator and printmaker. She received her BA in Graphic Design from the University of North Georgia in December of 2016. She has won several competitive awards and has showcased her work in both local and national exhibitions. Her time is well-spent creating art or in nature with her 7-year-old son. They live in a humble home in the foothills of the Appalachians.

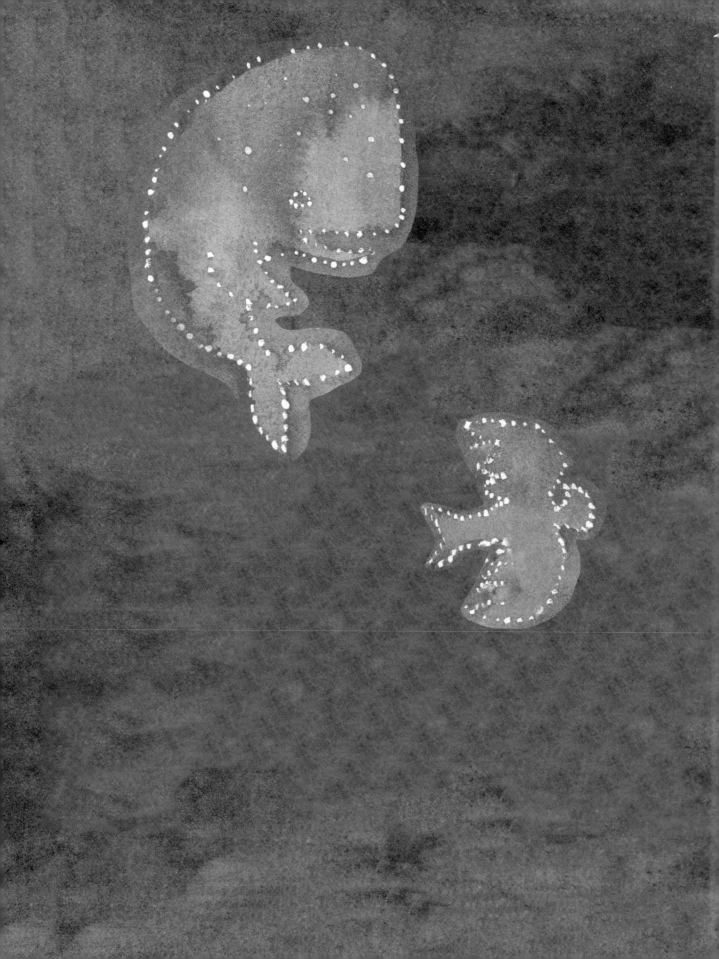